A CHAUTAUQUA IDYL

A CHAUTAUQUA IDYL

BY

GRACE LIVINGSTON HILL

Amereon
House

Dedicated to all of the ardent fans of Grace Livingston Hill who have kept alive her memory and spirit.

INTRODUCTORY NOTE

My Dear Mr. Lothrop: —

I have read Miss Livingston's little idyl with much pleasure. I cannot but think that if the older and more sedate members of the Chautauquan circles will read it, they will find that there are grains of profit in it; hidden grains, perhaps, but none the worse for being hidden at the first, if they only discover them. Miss Livingston has herself evidently understood the spirit of the movement in which the Chautauquan reading circles are engaged. That is more than can be said of everybody who expresses no opinion upon them. It is because she expresses no opinion, but rather tells, very simply, the story of the working out of the plan, that I am, glad you are going to publish her little poem: for poem it is, excepting that it is not in verse or in rhyme.

Believe me,

Very truly yours,

EDWARD EVERETT HALE

A CHAUTAUQUA IDYL was Grace Livingston Hill's first book, written and published under her maiden name at the age of 22. The introductory note on the previous page was written by Edward Everett Hale, a noted nineteenth century author and clergyman and a descendent of Edward Everett, orator and statesman, and of Nathan Hale, the martyr spy. The note, which was addressed to the publisher of A CHAUTAUQUA IDYL, expressed pleasure that the book was being published and praised Grace Livingston's perceptive interpretation of the spirit of the Chautauqua cultural series. She went on to produce more than 100 inspirational novels and stories over the next 60 years.

A CHAUTAUQUA IDYL

A CHAUTAUQUA IDYL

Down in a rocky pasture, on the edge of a wood, ran a little brook, tinkle, tinkle, over the bright pebbles of its bed. Close to the water's edge grew delicate ferns, and higher up the mossy bank nestled violets, blue and white and yellow.

Later in the fall the rocky pasture would glow with golden-rod and brilliant sumach, and ripe milk-weed pods would burst and fill the golden autumn sunshine with fleecy clouds. But now the nodding buttercups and smiling daisies held sway, with here and there a tall mullein standing sentinel.

It was a lovely place: off in the distance one could see the shimmering lake, to whose loving embrace the brook was forever hastening, framed by beautiful wooded hills, with a hazy purple mountain back of all.

But the day was not lovely. The clouds came down to the earth as near as they dared, scowling ominously. It was clear they had been drinking deeply. A sticky misty rain filled the air, and the earth looked sad, very sad.

The violets had put on their gossamers and drawn the hoods up over their heads, the ferns looked sadly drabbled, and the buttercups and daisies on the opposite bank, didn't even lean across to speak to their neighbors, but drew their yellow caps and white bonnets over their faces, drooped their heads and wished for the rain to be over. The wild roses over their faces, drooped their heads and wished for the rain to be over. The wild roses that grew near the bank hid under their leaves. The ferns went to sleep; even the trees leaned disconsolately over the brook and wished for the long rainy afternoon to be over, while little tired wet birds in their branches never stirred, nor even spoke to each other, but stood hour after hour on one foot, with their shoulders hunched up, and one eye shut.

At last a little white violet broke the damp stillness.

"O dear!" she sighed, "this is so tiresome, I wish we could do something nice. Won't some one please talk a little?"

No one spoke, and some of the older ferns even scowled at her, but little violet was not to be put down. She turned her hooded face on a tall pink bachelor button growing by her side.

This same pink button was a new-comer among them. He had been brought, a little brown seed, by a fat robin, early in the spring, and dropped down close by this sweet violet.

"Mr. Button," she said, "you have been

a great traveller. Won't you tell us some of your experiences?"

"Yes, yes; tell, tell, tell," babbled the brook.

The warm wind clapped him on the shoulder, and shook him gently, crying, — "Tell them, old fellow, and I'll fan them a bit, while you do it."

"Tell, tell," chirped the little birds overhead.

"O yes!" chorused the buttercups and daisies.

The little birds opened one eye and perked their heads in a listening attitude, and all the violets put their gossamer hoods behind their ears to that they might hear better.

"Well, I might tell you about Chautauqua," said pink bachelor thoughtfully.

"And what is Chautauqua?" questioned a saucy little fish who had stopped on his way to the lake to listen.

"Chautauqua is a place, my young friend, a beautiful place, where I spent last summer with my family," said the bachelor in a very patronizing tone.

"Oh! you don't say so," said the naughty

little fish with a grimace, and sped on his way to the lake, to laugh with all the other fishes at the queer new word.

"Go on, go on, go on," sang the brook.

"We lived in a garden by a house just outside the gates," began Bachelor.

"What gates?" interrupted the eager daisies.

"Why, the gates of the grounds."

"What grounds?"

"Why, the grounds of Chautauqua."

"But who is Chautauqua?" asked the puzzled violets.

"Don't you know? Chautauqua is a beautiful place in the woods, shut in from the world by a high fence all around it, with locked gates. It is on the shore of a lovely lake. Many people come there every year, and they have meetings, and they sing beautiful songs about birds and flowers and sky and water and God and angels and dear little babies and stars. Men come there from all over this world, and stand up and talk high, grand thoughts, and the people listen and wave their handkerchiefs till it looks like an orchard full of cherry trees in blossom.

"They have lovely singers — ladies who sing alone as sweet as birds, and they have grand choruses of song besides, by hundreds of voices. And they have instruments to play on — organs and pianos, and violins and harps."

"How beautiful," murmured the flowers.

"Tell us more," said the brook; "tell us more, more, more — tell, tell, tell!"

"More, more," said the wind.

"It lasts all summer, so the people who can't come at one time will come at another, though my cousin said she thought that one day all the people in the world came at once. There must have been something very grand to bring so many that day. There were not enough rooms for visitors to sleep in, and Chautauqua is a large place, the largest I was ever in. Yes," reflectively, "I think all the world must have been there."

The little white violet looked up.

"There was one day last summer when no one came through the pasture, and no one went by on the road, and all day long we saw not one person. It must have been that day, and they were all gone to Chautauqua," she said softly.

"I shouldn't wonder at all," said Bachelor.

Then they all looked sober and still. They were thinking. The idea that all the people in the world had come together for a day was very great to them.

At last one spoke.

"How nice it would be if all the flowers in the world would come together for a day," said the little violet.

"And all the birds," chirped a sparrow.

"And all the brooks and lakes and ocean," laughed the brook.

"And all the trees," sighed the tall elm.

"Oh! and all the winds. We could make as beautiful music as ever any organ or piano made."

"But what is it all for?" asked a bright-eyed daisy.

"To teach the people all about the things that the great God has made and show them how to live to please Him, and how to please Him, and how to please Him in the best way," promptly answered Bachelor.

"There is a great good man at the head of it, and I heard a lady say that God Himself sent him there to take care of Chautauqua for Him, for it is all made to praise God. They have schools, — everybody studies, but it is all about God that they learn, — about the things He made, or how to praise Him better, and all the talking — they call it lecturing, — is to help men to praise and love God more. They have three beautiful mottoes:

" 'We study the word and works of God.' 'Let us keep our Heavenly Father in our midst,' and, 'Never be discouraged.' "

"Wonderful, wonderful, wonderful," said the old forest tree.

"It is just what we need," piped one of the birds. "We don't praise God half enough. Here we've been sitting and sulking all the afternoon because it is raining, and never one thankful chirp have we given for all the yesterdays and yesterdays when it hasn't rained. We need a Chautauqua. I declare, I'm ashamed!" And he poured forth such a glad, thankful song of praise as thrilled the old forest trees through and through and most effectually waked the napping ferns.

"Yes," said the listening daisies when the song was done and the bird had stopped to rest his throat, "we need a Chautauqua."

"Let's have a Chautauqua!" cried the brook.

"But how could we," said the wise-eyed violet, "When we know so little about it?"

"I will tell you all I know," said Bachelor graciously. "You see we lived just outside the gates, and people used often to come and buy my brothers and sisters. Once a young man came and bought a very large bunch of them and took them to a young lady in a white dress, and she wore them everywhere for three or four days — you know our family is a very long-lived one, and we are something like the camel, in that we can go a long time without a drink of water — well, she kept them carefully and took them everywhere she went, and they saw and heard a great many new things. One evening this young lady sat in a big place full of people, and an old lady sitting behind her said to another lady, 'Just see those pink bachelor buttons! My mother used to have some just like them growing in her garden, years and years ago, and I haven't seen any since.' The young lady heard her, turned around and gave her a whole handful of my brothers and sisters. After the meeting was out, the old lady carried them away with her, but one slipped out of her hand and fell on the walk, and some one came along in the darkness and crushed her. Quite early the next morning our neighbor, Mr. Robin, going to the market for a worm for breakfast, saw her lying in this sad state, and with great difficulty brought her home to us. She lived only a day or two longer, but long enough to tell us many of her experiences.

"After she had faded and gone, our friend Robin went every day to hear and see what was going on inside the great gates, and every night when the bells were ringing" —

"What bells?" interrupted an impolite buttercup.

"The night bells for the people to go to sleep by. They rang beautiful music on bells by the water to put the people to sleep, and in the morning to wake them, and they had bells to call them to the big place to praise God, and hear the lectures and singing."

"Beautiful, beautiful," murmured the brook.

"And every night," proceeded the bachelor, "when the bells were ringing we would wake up and Robin would tell us all about the day inside the gates. Of course I can't remember all I know."

"Perhaps I can help you a little," spoke out an old fish who had come up the stream unobserved some time before. "I lived in Lake Chautauqua myself for some years until my daughter sent for me to come and live with her in yonder lake."

They all looked at the old fish with great veneration, and thanked him kindly.

"Well, how shall we begin?" said an impatient daisy.

"I should think the first thing to be done is to make a motion that we have a Chautauqua," Bachelor said.

Then rose up a tall old fern. "I make a motion to that effect."

"I second it," chirped a sparrow.

"All in favor of the motion say 'aye,' " said Bachelor, in a deep, important voice.

And then arose such a chorus of "aye's" as never was heard before in that grove. The wind blew it, the brook gurgled it, the great forest trees waved it, all the little flowers filled the air with their perfumed voices, the far-off lake murmured its assent, the purple mountain nodded its weary old head, the sun shot triumphantly through the dark clouds, and all God's works seemed joining in the "aye, aye, aye," that echoed from hillside to wood.

"A unanimous vote, I think" said Bachelor, after the excitement had somewhat subsided.

"The next question is, When shall we have it?"

"Oh! right away, of course," nodded a buttercup. "See! the sun has come out to help us."

"But," objected white Violet, "we can't. We must invite all the flowers and birds and brooks and trees all over the world, and they will have to get ready. It will take the flowers the rest of the summer and all of next winter to get their dresses made and packed in their brown travelling seed trunks. I'm sure it would me if I were to go away from here for the summer, and it is late in the season already. We couldn't get word to them all in time."

"Yes," said the fish, "and there are the travelling expenses to be arranged for such a large company. We should have to secure reduced rates. They always do on Chautauqua Lake."

"Oh! as to that," said the wind, "I and the birds would do the transportation free of charge, and the brook would do all it could, I'm sure."

"Of course, of course," babbled the brook.

"That is very kind of you indeed," said Bachelor. "But I should think that the earliest possible beginning that we could hope to have would be next spring."

After much impatient arguing on the part of the buttercups and daisies, it was finally agreed that the first meeting of their Chautauqua should be held the following spring.

"It must last all summer," they said, "because some of us can come early and some late. There is the golden-rod now, it never can come till late in the fall."

"Of course, of course; certainly, certainly, certainly," chattered the brook.

"What comes next?" softly asked the

wild rose.

"The next thing to do is to appoint a committee to make out the programme," remarked the fish.

"Committee! Who is that?" cried a butterfly.

"Programme! what's programme?" chirped a sparrow.

"O dear! we need a dictionary," sighed the roses.

"What's a dictionary?" asked a little upstart of a fern.

"Silence!" sternly commanded Bachelor. "Will Miss Rose kindly explain the meaning of dictionary, after which Mr. Fish will proceed to tell us about programme and committee."

Little Rose blushed all over her pretty face, and after thinking a moment, replied —

"A dictionary is a book that tells what all words mean."

"Oh!" sighed the wind, "we must have a dictionary."

Mr. Fish having made a dash up stream after a fly, now resumed his sedate manner and spoke.

"My friends, a programme says what we will have every day, and a committee are the ones who make it."

"Then let's all be committee," said the buttercup.

That's a very good plan," said Bachelor. "Now, what shall we have? They always have a prayer meeting first at Chautauqua."

"We can all pray," said the elm. "Let us have a prayer meeting first every morning to thank the dear God for the new day, and let the rising sun be the leader."

"That is good," said the flowers, and bright rays of light, the sun's little children, kissed them tenderly.

"What is next?"

"They have a large choir, and every morning after the prayer meeting they meet and practice with the great organ and piano and band."

"We will be the singers," chorused the birds.

"I will tinkle, tinkle like a piano," sang the brook, "tinkle, tinkle, tinkle, — "

"I will play the band, for I have very many instruments at my command, and my friend the thunder will play the organ, while you, dear old trees, shall be my violins and harps, and every morning we will practice," said the wind.

"What do they have next at Chautauqua?" asked a pert blackbird.

"Lectures," said the fish.

"What are lectures?"

"Talks about things."

"What things?"

"Oh! evolution and literature and theology and philosophy and art and poetry and science, and a great many other things."

The high-sounding words rolled out from that fish's mouth as if he actually thought he understood them.

Silence reigned for a few minutes, deep and intense, at last broken by the white violet:

"We never could have all those, for we

don't know anything about them. And who could talk about such things? None of us."

Silence again. They were all thinking earnestly.

"I don't believe it. Not one word," chattered a saucy squirrel. "That's a fish story. As if *you* could get on dry land and go to lectures."

"Oh! very well, you needn't believe it if you don't want to," answered the fish in a hurt tone, "but I heard a man on board the steamer read the programme, and those are the very words he read."

"If we only had a dictionary," again sighed the rose.

"Dictionary, dictionary, dic, dic, dictionary," murmured the brook, thoughtfully.

"A dictionary is absolutely necessary before we can proceed any further," said the south wind. "And as I am obliged to travel to New York this evening, I will search everywhere, and if possible bring one back with me. Anything can be had in New York. It is getting late, and I think we had better adjourn to meet again tomorrow. I hope to be able to return by two o'clock. In the meantime, let us all think deeply of what we have heard, and if any one can see a way out of our difficulty, let him tell us then."

The sunbeams kissed the flowers good-night, the forest trees waved farewell to the good wind, the brook called, "Good-night! sweet dreams till tomorrow, tomorrow, tomorrow," and all the air was soft with bird vespers.

Into the bright sunshine of the next afternoon came the winds and the eager birds to the place on the bank where the violets grew.

The daisies leaned far over the bank to listen.

The South wind came bringing two or three torn sheets of an old dictionary.

"It is all I could find, and I've had hard work to get this," said he. "I went in at a window where lay an open dictionary — I had no idea that a dictionary was such a very large book. — It was an old one, so I had no trouble in tearing out these few leaves, as the paper was so tender. I took them out of the window and hid them in a safe place and went back for more, but just as I was turning the leaves over to find evolution, some one came up and shut the window, and I had to crawl out through the cracks. Well, I have all the 'P's' and some of the 'T's'; we can find theology and poetry.

"Philosophy, too," said wise Violet.

"My dear, that is spelled with an 'f'," said the kind old wind patronizingly.

"O, no! I am sure you are mistaken. It is 'p-h-i-l'; look and see if I am not right."

The wind slowly turned over the leaves of his meagre dictionary, and, sure enough, there it was, — "p-h-i-l-o-s-o-p-h-y."

"Is it there? What does it say?" questioned the eager flowers.

"Philosophy, the love of or search after, wisdom," slowly read the wind.

"Oh!" said the flowers, "is that all it is? Why, we know philosophy."

"I think the forest trees could lecture on philosophy," said the wind.

"Yes, yes, yes," they all cried. "The forest trees, for they are very old and have had longer to search for wisdom than we."

"Very well; three lectures a week on philosophy, by the old forest trees; write it down, please," cried Bachelor.

The Secretary, a scarlet-headed woodpecker, carefully carved it on the trunk of an old tree, and I think you can still find the minutes of that day written in lines of beauty all over the tree.

"Theology is the next word," announced the wind, and again turned over the leaves of their precious dictionary.

"The science of God," he read. "Science, what is science? If we only had the 's's'!"

"I know what it is," chirped a bird. I hopped into the schoolhouse this morning, and a book was open on the desk, and no one was there, so I hopped up and took a look to see if there was anything in it to help us. The first words my eye fell on were these, — 'science is knowledge.' And I didn't wait for any more, but flew away to sit in a tree and say it over so that I wouldn't forget it. Going back a little later to see if I could get any more words, I found the schoolhouse full of dreadful boys. As I flew away again, this little piece of paper blew out of the window, and I brought it, thinking it might be helpful."

As he finished speaking, he deposited a small fragment of a definition spelling-book at the foot of the elm tree, and flew up into the branches again, for he was a bashful bird, and this was a very long speech for him to make before so many.

"Good, good, good," cried all the committee.

"To go back to theology," said the wind. "It is the science of God. Science is knowledge, therefore theology is knowledge of God. That is a very great thing. Who is able to lecture on the knowledge of God?"

Silence all. No one dared to volunteer. None felt worthy to do so great a thing.

Out spoke a shy little wren. "Last night I slept in a notch close over a church window, and the window was open and there was a meeting of the people there and the minister read out of the Bible these words: 'The heavens declare the glory of God, and the firmament sheweth his handiwork.' "

She paused a moment to gather courage, and then said, "Why couldn't the heavens teach theology?"

"Bless your heart, little wren, that is the very thing," cried the blustering north wind. And all the flowers cried, — "The heavens shall teach theology!"

The sky bowed its assent and said, "I will do my best to perform the wonderful work entrusted to me."

And the happy brook murmured, "Glory, glory, glory! the glory of God."

"Now we will see what this bit of paper has for us," said the wind as he picked up the paper at the foot of the elm.

"Ah! What have we here? Evolution! Just what we want: 'evolution, the act of unfolding or unrolling.' "

He stopped with a thoughtful look.

"Yes, I see. As the young leaves and flowers unfold. The plants must take full charge of this department, I think. I remember once turning over the leaves of a fat, dark-gray book, with gilt letters on its back. It lay on a minister's window-seat, and it looked interesting, so I read a few minutes while the minister was out and not using it, and among other things that I read was this, and it stayed with me ever since: 'A lily grows mysteriously. Shaped into beauty by secret and invisible fingers, the flower develops, we know not how. Every day the thing is done: it is God.' You see, my dear," addressing himself to a pure white lily that had only that morning unfolded its delicate petals to the sun, "you see a great many don't understand how it is done. You need to tell how God has made you able to unfold."

"Yes, we will, we can," they all cried.

"The flowers will speak on Evolution," wrote down Woodpecker.

"There are three more words spoken by our friend Fish, still unexplained, — literature, — "

"I know what literature means, Mr. Wind, it is books," announced a bright butterfly who had just arrived on the scene.

"Are you sure?" questioned the fish doubtfully.

"Yes, of course I am. I went with a big pinchbug one day into a great room full of books, and he said, when he saw the shelves and shelves full of them, 'My! what a lot of literature!' "

The committee looked convinced, but now came the question of books, — Where should they get them? How could they lecture on books, when they knew nothing about them?

"We must just send word around to all the flowers and birds and trees and everything, to see who can lecture on books, and we must all keep our eyes and ears open," said a buttercup bud.

"We shall have to lay that on the table for the present," said the wind.

"But we haven't any table," chattered a squirrel.

"A well brought-up squirrel should know better than to interrupt. We shall have to put this aside, then, until we can learn more about it. In the meantime, let us proceed with the next word on the list, poetry."

"I know," said the brook. "A bit of paper lay upon my bank, miles and miles away from here, too high up for me to reach, but I could read it. It said, 'For poetry is the blossom and the fragrance of all human knowledge.' And I have said it over and over all the way here."

"Ah! the flowers shall give us poetry," said the good old wind.

Bachelor bowed his head and said, "We will try."

"Try, try, try," chattered the brook.

"Art is next, I believe," said Bachelor.

"Yes, art," said a squirrel.

"Art is making pictures," said the moss.

"Then the sunset must paint them, for there are no pictures made like those of the sunset," said the wind.

The sun hastened to mix his paint, and in answer to the request that he would be professor of art, painted one of the most glorious sunset scenes that mortal eye has ever looked upon. Rapidly he dashed on the color, delicate greens and blues blending with the sea-shell pink, and glowing with deep crimson and gold, till the assembled committee fairly held their breaths with delight. The crimson and gold and purple in the west were beginning to fade and mix with soft greys and tender yellows, before the committee thought of returning to their work.

"What a lot of time we have wasted," said the oldest squirrel; "Tomorrow is Sunday, and of course we can't work then, and now it is time to go home."

"Not wasted, dear squirrel," said White

Violet, "not wasted when we were looking at God's beautiful sunset."

Bachelor looked down at her in all her sweetness and purity, and some of the flowers say that later when he went to bid her good-night he kissed her.

"Tomorrow being Sunday reminds me that we have not made any arrangements for our Sunday sermons. They always have great sermons at Chautauqua, and I have often heard the passengers on the steamer scolding because the boats did not run on Sunday, for they said the great men always kept their best thoughts for sermons." This from the fish.

They all paused. "Why can't any of us preach sermons, what shall we do?" questioned a fern.

"I'm sure I don't know; we might each of us go to church and listen to a sermon and preach it over again," said a thoughtful bird.

"But we couldn't remember it all, and by next summer we would have forgotten it entirely," said one more cautious.

"Well, we must go," said the wind. "Monday we will consider these subjects. To-morrow is God's day, and we must go immediately, for it is getting dark."

And so they all rested on the Sabbath day, and praised the great God, and never a wee violet, not even a chattering chipmunk, allowed his thoughts to wander off to the programme for the next summer, but gave their thoughts to holy things.

The busy Monday's work was all done up, and the committee gathered again, waiting for the work to go on, when there came flying in great haste, a little bluebird, and, breathless, stopped on a branch to rest a moment ere he tried to speak.

"What is the matter?" they all cried.

"Were you afraid you would be late? You ought not to risk your health; it is not good to get so out of breath," said a motherly old robin.

"Oh! I have such good news to tell you," cried the little bird as soon as he could speak. "I sat on a bough this morning, close to a window where sat an old lady, who was reading aloud to a sick man, so I stopped to listen. These are the words she read, — 'Sermons in stones, books in running brooks.' I didn't hear any more, but came right away to study that. I was so glad I had found something to help us. Two things in one."

They all looked very much amazed.

"Why, we didn't think we could do anything!" cried the stones, "and here we can do one of the best things there is to be done. Thank the dear God for that. We will preach sermons full of God and his works, for we have seen a great many ages, and their story is locked up in us."

"And the brook shall tell us of books," said the old wind. "There is good in everything, and we shall try not to feel discouraged the next time we are in a difficulty."

"Books in running brooks," said the brook. "Books, books, books. And I too can praise Him."

"This morning," said a sober-looking bird, "a small girl just under my nest in the orchard, was saying something over and over to herself, and I listened; and these were the words that she said:

"The ocean looketh up to heaven as 'twere a living thing,
The homage of its waves is given in ceaseless worshipping
They kneel upon the sloping sand, as bends the human knee,

A beautiful and tireless hand, the priesthood
    of the sea,
They pour the glittering treasures out which
    in the deep have birth,
And chant their awful hymns about the
    watching hills of earth."

"If the ocean is so good and grand as
that he ought to do something at our Chautauqua. Couldn't he? God must love him very
much, he worships him so much."

"Yes," said the elm tree. "I have heard
that a great man once said, 'God, God, God
walks on thy watery rim.' "

"Wonderful, glorious," murmured the
flowers.

"They tell stories at Chautauqua — pretty stories about things and people; and I have
heard that Ocean has a wonderful story. We
might send word to ask if he will tell it,"
suggested Bachelor.

"I fear he cannot leave home," said the
wind, "but we might try him."

So it was agreed that the wood-pecker
should write a beautiful letter, earnestly in-
viting him to take part in the grand new movement for the coming summer. The brook
agreed to carry the daintily-carved missive to

the lake, and the lake to the river, and the river would carry it to the sea.

Bachelor spoke next: "They have a School of Languages at Chautauqua, could we have one?"

"I have thought of that," said the fish, "but who could teach it?"

"That is the trouble," said Bachelor, slowly shaking his head.

"I know," said a little bird. "I went to church last night and heard the Bible read, and it said, 'Day unto day uttereth speech, and night unto night sheweth knowledge. There is no speech nor language where their voice is not heard.' I think the day and the night could teach the School of Languages."

"The day and the night, the day and the night," said the brook.

"Yes," said the oldest tree of all, "the day and the night know all languages."

"We must have a Missionary Day and a Temperance Day," said the wise old fish.

"What is a Temperance Day?" asked a young squirrel, who was not yet very well acquainted with the questions of the day.

"My dear," said his mother, "there are some bad people in the world who make vile stuff and give it to people to drink, and it makes them sick and cross; then they do not please God, and there are some good people who are trying to keep the bad people from making it, and the others from drinking it; they are called Temperance."

"Oh!" said the squirrel, "but why do the folks drink it? I should think they'd know better."

"So should I, but they don't. Why, my dear, I must tell you of something that happened to me once. I lived in a tree at a summer resort, that year, and just under my bough was a window; a young man roomed there for a few days, and every morning he would come to the window with a black bottle in his hand, and pour out some dark stuff and mix sugar and water with it, and drink it as if he thought it was very good. I watched him for several mornings, and one morning the bell rang while he was drinking, and he left the glass on the window-sill, and went to breakfast. I hopped down to see what it was and it smelled good, so I tasted it. I liked the taste pretty well, so I drank all there was left. Then I started home, but, will you believe it? I could not walk straight, and very soon I could hardly stand up. I tried to climb up a tree, but fell off the first bough, and there I lay for a long, long time. When I awoke I had such a terrible pain in my head! All that day I suffered, and didn't get over my bad feelings for several days. I tell this as a warning to you, that you may never be tempted to touch anything to drink but water, my dear."

"You must tell that story, Mrs. Squirrel," said Bachelor. "And we will call it a story of intemperance, by one of its victims."

"I will, with all my heart, if it will do any one any good," she responded.

"Yes, we must have a Temperance Day and all make a speech on drinking cold water," said the fish.

"And dew," said the violet.

"I have always drank water, and never anything else, and I think one could scarcely find an older or a healthier tree than I am," said the elm.

"That is true," said the fish.

"Cold water, cold water, cold water," babbled the brook.

"Yes, we can all speak on Temperance Day; we will have a great platform meeting. That is what they call it at Chautauqua when a great many speak about one thing. I heard a man telling his little girl about it on the boat," said the fish.

And the woodpecker wrote it down.

"What was that other you said?" asked a sharp little chipmunk.

"Missionary Day," said the fish.

"And what is that?"

"Why, there are home missions and foreign missions," said the fish. "And they talk about them both. I think they have a day for each, or maybe two or three. Missions are doing good to some one, but I don't exactly see the difference between home and foreign missions."

"Why, that is plain to me," said Bachelor. "Home missions is when some one does something kind to you, and foreign missions is when you do something kind to some one else."

"Of course; why didn't I think of that before?" said the fish.

"One day last year I was very hungry," said a robin, "very hungry and cold. I had come on too early in the season. There came a cold snap, and the ground was frozen. I could find nothing at all to eat. I was almost frozen myself, and had begun to fear that my friends would come on to find me starved to death instead of getting ready for them as they expected. But a little girl saw me and threw some crumbs out of the window. I went and ate them, and every day as long as the cold weather lasted she threw me crumbs — such good ones too — some of them cake; and she gave me silk ravelings to make my nest of. I think that was a home mission, don't you?"

"Yes, my dear, it was," said Bachelor.

"You might tell that as one thing," said the wind.

"I will," said Birdie.

Said a daisy, "When I was very thirsty, one day, and the clouds sent down no good rain, the dear brook jumped up high here, and splashed on me so I could drink, and I think that was a home mission."

"Yes, yes," said the elm, "it was."

"I know a story I could tell," said the ferns.

"And I," said the elm; "one of many years ago, when I was but a little twig."

"I know a home mission story too," said White Violet.

"And I," said the brook. "Once I was almost all dried up and could hardly reach the lake, and a dear lovely spring burst up and helped me along until the dry season was over."

"And I, and I," chorused a thousand voices.

"But what about foreign missions?" said the fish.

"I sang a beautiful song to a sad old lady in a window, this morning," said a mocking-bird.

"That's foreign missions," said the chipmunk.

"Some naughty boys had another boy's hat yesterday, and I found it for him and blew it to his feet," said the wind.

"I sent a bunch of buds to a sick girl, this morning," said the rose-bush with a blush.

"I think we shall have no lack of foreign missions," remarked Bachelor.

"But what can *we* do?" asked an old

gray squirrel. "We can't preach, nor teach. We can run errands and carry messages, but that isn't much."

"You might be on the commissary department," said the wind.

"What's that?" they all asked.

"Things to eat. We shall need a great many, and you could all lay in a stock of nuts, enough to last all summer, for a great many."

"Why, surely!" they cried, and all that fall such a hurrying and scurrying from bough to bough there was as never was seen before. They worked very hard, storing up nuts, and the people came near not getting any at all.

It must have been a week from the time they sent their letter to Old Ocean, that one afternoon as they were assembled, waiting for the decision of a certain little committee, which had been sent over behind a stone to decide who should be the leader of the choir, that up the stream came a weary little fish.

He was unlike any fish that had ever been seen in that brook, and caused a great deal of remark among the flowers before he was within hearing distance.

He came wearily, as though he had travelled a long distance, but as he drew nearer, the old fish exclaimed, "There comes a salt-water fish! perhaps he has a message from the ocean."

Then the little company were all attention.

Nearer and nearer he came, and stopped before the old fish with a low bow, inquiring whether this was the Chautauqua Committee.

On being told that it was, he laid a bit of sea-weed, a pearly shell, and a beautiful stem of coral upon the bank, and said: "I have a message from Old Ocean for you. He sends you greetings and many good wishes for the success of your plan, and regrets deeply that he cannot be with you next summer; but he is old, very old, and he has so much to do that he cannot leave even for a day or two. If he should the world would be upside down. There would be no rain in the brooks, the lakes would dry up, and the crops and the people all would die."

"O dear! and we should die too," said the flowers.

"Yes, you would die, too," said the salt-water fish.

"He has a great many other things besides to take care of; there are the great ships to carry from shore to shore, and there is the telegraph, — "

"What is telegraph?" interrupted that saucy little squirrel who had no regard even for a stranger's presence.

"Telegraph is a big rope that people send letters to their friends on. It is under the water in the ocean, and the letters travel so fast that we have never yet been able to see them, though we have watched night and day."

"Wonderful, strange," they all murmured.

"Old Ocean says," proceeded the messenger, "that he cannot give you all of his story, as it would be too long, but that he sends some of it written on this shell, and in this coral and in this bit of sea-weed. In the shell is a drop of pure salt water that if carefully examined will tell you many more wonderful things."

They all thanked the fish kindly for coming so far to bring them these treasures, and begged him to stay and rest, but he declined, saying he had a family at home and must hasten, so he turned to go.

"Stay!" cried Bachelor. "Wouldn't you be willing to come next summer and give us a lecture on the telegraph?"

The fish laughed.

"Bless you!" said he, "I couldn't do that. I don't know enough about it myself. Ask the lightning. He is the head manager, and will give you all the lectures you want. Goodby! the sun is getting low, and I must be off." And he sped away, leaving the woodpecker writing down "telegraph" and "lightning" on the corner of his memoranda.

And now the committee returned, having decided, by unanimous vote, that the mocking-bird should be the leader of the choir, as he could sing any part, and so help along the weak ones whenever he could see the need of it.

There was a pause after the committee had been told all that had happened during their absence, broken at last by Bachelor.

"I've been thinking," said he, "that it might be as well for us to have a reply to Ingersoll."

"What is that?" they asked, for they were getting used to strange things, and did not seem so surprised at the new word.

"Ingersoll is a man that says there is no God and he has written a great many things to prove it," said Bachelor gravely.

The other poor little flowers were too much shocked to say anything, and they all looked at one another dumbly.

"Is he blind," asked a bird.

"He must know better," asserted a fern. "No one could possibly believe such a thing."

"I don't know whether he is blind, but I think not," said Bachelor. "They say he has made a great many other people believe as he does because he talks so beautifully."

"How dreadful!" said the flowers in a sad voice.

"They had a man at Chautauqua who answered all he said and proved that it was untrue, but every one did not hear him. I think we ought to have a day to answer Ingersoll," again said Bachelor.

"Yes, we must," said the north wind; "and we will all prove there *is* a God. No one could have made me but God." And he blew and blew until the flowers crouched down almost afraid at his fierceness.

When all was quiet again, out hopped a dignified looking bird. "My friends," said he, "my wife and I went to church last night, and they sang a beautiful hymn that has long been one of my favorites. I told my wife to listen hard, and this morning, with my help, she was able to sing it. I think it would help on this subject if we were to sing it for you now."

"Sing, sing, sing," said the brook.

The meek little wife at her husband's word stepped out, and together they sang this wonderful hymn:

The spacious firmament on high,
With all the blue ethereal sky,
The spangled heavens, a shining frame,
Their great original proclaim;
The unwearied sun, from day to day,
Does his creator's power display,
And publishes to every land
The work of an almighty hand.

Soon as the evening shades prevail,
The moon takes up the wondrous tale,
And nightly to the listening earth
Repeats the story of her birth:
While all the stars that round her burn,

And all the planets in their turn,
Confirm the tidings as they roll,
And spread the truth from pole to pole.

What though, in solemn silence, all
Move round the dark, terrestrial ball?
What though no REAL voice or sound
Amid their radiant orbs be found?

In REASON'S ear they all rejoice,
And utter forth a glorious voice,
Forever singing as they shine,
The hand that made us is divine.

When they had finished, the whole congregation bowed their heads.

"Yes," they said, "every day we will show forth the greatness of God who made us, and that bad man will see and hear and believe, and the people will not be led away from God any more."

"We will make that our great aim, to show forth the glory of God," they all cried together.

So the little workers planned, and sent their messengers far and wide, over land and sea, and made out their programme; and the lecturers spent days and days preparing their manuscript, — for aught I know they are at it yet.

The flowers all have received their invitations to come, and some were so eager to be off that they packed their brown seed trunks and coaxed the wind to carry them immediately, that they might be early on the spot.

Next spring when the snow is gone and the trees are putting forth their leaves, and all looks tender and beautiful, you will see the birds flying back and forth, very busy, carrying travellers and messages; the squirrels will go chattering to their store-houses to see that all is right, and to air the rooms a little; the birds will build many nests, more than they need, and you will wonder why, and will never know that they are summer nests for rent, else you might like to rent one yourself.

The wind, too, will be busy, so busy that he will barely have time to dry your clothes that hang out among the apple blossoms.

You don't know what it all means?

Wake up quite early every morning and listen, Be patient and one morning, just as the first pink glow of the rising sun tinges the east, you will hear a watching tree call out, —

The year's at the spring,
And the day's at the morn;
Morning's at seven;
The hillside's dew pearled;
The lark's on the wing;
The snail's on the thorn;
God's in his heaven —
All's right with the world.

And then all the lily-bells will chime out the call to prayer, the great red sun will come up and lead, and the little Chautauqua will open.

You will hear the sweet notes of praise from the bird choir, and prayers will rise from the flowers like sweet incense; you will see and hear it all, but will you remember that it is all to show forth the glory of God?